CW81086254

Praise for Brian Brackbrick and the Hazard of Harry Hatman

"This is a really good book with adventure and mischief lurking round every corner. I really enjoyed the book because you never know what's about to happen. When they come out, I can't wait to read the other books." (Solomon, aged 9)

"This book is brilliant. I bought this book for my grandson – he absolutely loved the book and to be honest so did I. We can't wait for the next one." (Kevin, a grown-up)

"Brian Brackbrick is an <u>awesome</u> book...I'm so excited for the next book in this series! Well done!" (Archie, aged 9)

"I thought it was awesome and I really enjoyed it. All the characters were fun and I liked George Bum." (Jake, aged 6)

"A lovely, easy to read book for younger readers wanting something a little bit longer." (BB Taylor, a grown-up on the outside)

Praise for Brian Brackbrick and the Mystery of Mrs Blumenhole

"After reading book 1 with my class, we were desperately awaiting book 2 and it didn't disappoint! These books are just perfect for this age group. I would definitely recommend for teachers and parents alike." (Miss Clapp, Terrific Teacher)

"I love Brian Brackbrick. It makes me want to read more because it is a mystery." (Jacob C., aged 7)

"I love bonkers fun, and Brian Brackbrick's adventures are that and more! Dare you discover Mrs Blumenhole's secret?" (Kate Wiseman, Sensational Storyteller)

"My favourite character is George Bum. I think they are very clever and will find out what has happened." (Lily, aged 7)

"My favourite element was the creative plants found in Mrs. Blumenhole's shop which gave the impression they could have originated from a Rowling Herbology class or the exquisite mind of Dahl...This was another fun and fabulous book that delivered on every level and I can't wait to see what happens next." (Stacy Walton, Brilliant Book Blogger)

"Brian Brackbrick makes it cool to be clever." (Sacha, aged 7).

Praise for Brian Brackbrick and the Scowl of the Scorpion

"I love how Brian and George work together to solve the mysteries and story keeps you on your toes wanting more. I can't wait for the next one!"
(Alfie, aged 8)

"Witty, clever and completely for children. No pomp and ceremony to appeal to adults. Just pure fun and excitement for children. Isn't that what reading for pleasure is all about?"
(Ceridwen Eccles, Terrific Teacher)

"I like your book because it has a bit of adventure, suspense and funny parts. Looking forward to the next book!"
(Capri, aged 8)

"A true triumph. It's witty, snappy and entertaining to boot and perfect for all our young readers out there. Another great addition to an already spectacular series." (Stacy Walton, Brilliant Book Blogger)

"Such a fun premise, with a great message!" (Kathryn Evans, Awesome Author)

Praise for Brian Brackbrick and the Melody of Morris Hawkwind

"I really liked book 4 because there's a whole bunch of mysteries. I can't wait to see who Mr Sparker is!"

(Lottie, aged 8)

"I love it, it's all about a boy who is a master detective. The books are funny and mysterious!"

(George, aged 11)

"This book is a sensation! It grips you from the very beginning and keeps you captivated throughout. It's witty, fun and a masterclass in engaging younger readers. I look forward to the next one!"

(Shannen Doherty, Terrific Teacher)

"This is a great book! My brother and I have read them all and we laughed so much!" (Ottilie, aged 10)

"It is funny and a fab detective story. You don't know what will happen next!" (Olivia, aged 10)

"What a fun read! I read it as a bedtime story with my son and we were both thoroughly entertained. The cleverly written characters were engaging and memorable and it's a really absorbing story. I would highly recommend for children of all ages!"

(Lacey Dearie, Brilliant Blogger and Author)

"I found the book good, fun and interesting. And that the letters were big made it easy to read."

(Isabella, aged 8)

"This is a marvellously musical story full of mischief and mishap that hits all the right notes."

(Gareth P. Jones, Awesome Author and Magical Musician)

"Interesting, had good words in it."

(Jairaj, aged 9)

"Hilarious, perfect for all primary aged children who will fall in love with these amazing books!"

(Eleanor, aged 11)

"I liked the book because it was fun to read."

(Alfie, aged 8)

"Fun and imaginative!"

(Ellis, aged 8)

Praise for Brian Brackbrick and the Revelation of Raymond Rings

"I like how the book keeps me guessing until the very end!"
(Capri, aged 10)

"These are great books for young readers and book 5 continues the story brilliantly. Early readers need chapter books which introduce them to slightly more complex storylines and these books do that so well. They have fun characters and each book is a story in itself, as well as continuing the wider storyline of the series. Young readers will love this new instalment!"
(Miss Clapp, Terrific Teacher)

"The plot thickens in this next instalment! Perfect humour for children and adults. Kids will be hanging off their seats desperate to find out how things are resolved!"

(Rachel Campling, Amazing Author)

For Wilfred,
Thanks for
reading!

for Wilfred,
thanks for
reading!

Brian Brackbrick and the

Menace of Mr Sparker

Book 6 of 6

Copyright © 2021 by Dr. Garry R. Dix

ISBN-10: 8788921853

ISBN-13: 979-8788921853

For DYLAN, OLLIE and OWEN

We did it!

People!

Brian Brackbrick

George Bum

Fancy Nancy Sprinkle

Dr. Harley Letters

Sgt. Shelley Shiplap

Frankie Featherface

Mrs. Blumenhole

Old Mr. Hatson

Mr. Brackbrick

Mrs. Brackbrick

Harry Hatman

Mr. Carl Scorpion

Morris Hawkwind

Raymond Rings

Mr. Sparker

Places!

The Library

The Cake Shop

The Music Shop

The Police Station

Things!

Mysterious Gold Ring

Woolly Hat

Hawkwind Radio Transmitter

Simon the Scorpion

Super Giant Mega Cake Mixer

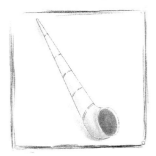

Giant Alpine Horn

ALSO BY THE AUTHOR

Brian Brackbrick and the Hazard of Harry Hatman

Brian Brackbrick and the Mystery of Mrs Blumenhole

Brian Brackbrick and the Scowl of the Scorpion

Brian Brackbrick and the Melody of Morris Hawkwind

Brian Brackbrick and the Revelation of Raymond Rings

Brian Brackbrick and George Bum have defeated Harry Hatman, rescued Old Mr. Hatston, stopped Carl Scorpion and his plague of scorpions, switched off Hawkwind Radio, stopped Raymond Rings, and proved that Morris Hawkwind is innocent. After giving Brian Brackbrick and George Bum another medal each, Lord Mayor Spencer reveals that his real name is Spencer Sparker — he is really Mr. Sparker, the villain who has been trying to take over the town!

Spencer Sparker uses his special mayor's hat and the control rings (except one...) to take control of all the people in the town, and sends them after Brian Brackbrick, who has the remaining control ring in his pocket...

CHAPTER 1:

BRIAN AND GEORGE

ON THE RUN!

"Run, George! Run!" shouted Brian.

Brian Brackbrick and George Bum both turned to run away, their new medals swinging from side-to-side around their necks. All the people of the town – who were being controlled by Mr. Sparker thanks to Raymond Rings' special jewellery – were slowly shuffling towards them with their arms outstretched, reaching for them. The people were slow, but there were so many of them! They circled around so that Brian and George had to **dodge** between, scramble under, and run around, in order to escape.

There were moments when a hand reached for them and Brian or George would **dodge** out of the way just in time, only to look up and see the blank, hypnotised face of one of their friends, such as Dr. Harley Letters, or Fancy Nancy, or Frankie Featherface, or even their parents. Every one of them was under Mr. Sparker's control.

Brian and George somehow made it through the crowd and ran off down the street; all the people, acting as one, turned to follow.

"What should we do, Brian?" asked George, who was trying not to panic.

"I do not know yet!" Brian exclaimed, as they came to a halt a safe distance from the crowd. Without meaning to, they had run towards the swimming pool, and they would be trapped if they carried on in that direction.

Meanwhile, the crowd of people slowly shuffled closer…

"We could hide in the swimming pool," George suggested. "In the changing rooms? In the car park?"

"I suspect they will find us wherever we hide. But how do they know how to follow us? Look at their blank faces."

George Bum looked at the faces of the people in the crowd, which were getting closer and closer.

"They're getting closer and closer, Brian!"

"They are being controlled by Mr. Sparker, so they are not thinking for themselves," said Brian thoughtfully, "but somehow they know where we are."

Brian moved to the other side of the road, pulling George with him. The people in the crowd copied them, all bumping into each other as they tried to move to the same side.

Brian then moved back to the other side, again pulling George with him, and the people in the crowd all copied them again.

"It is like they are following a signal," said Brian, "but where is the signal coming from?"

George could barely contain himself. "Brian, maybe it's – "

"Yes, in a moment, George," Brian interrupted. "Now, could Mr. Sparker have given us something without us realising it?"

"Yes, I think he did! It's the – "

"We do not have time, George, they are nearly here! We must work out how they are all following us."

"It's the medals, Brian!" shouted George Bum. "These big, heavy medals that Mr. Sparker gave us! It must be the medals!"

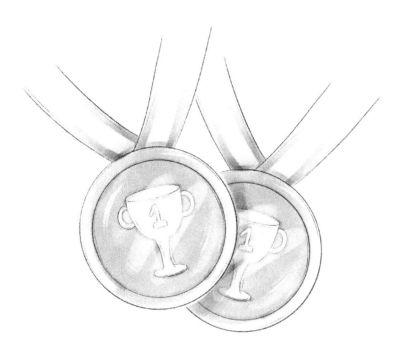

"Ah, yes, the medals," said Brian. "That is what I was going to say."

"Let's get rid of them, Brian!" George said as he started to take the medal from around his neck.

"Wait, George, I have an idea! If we run down the little street behind the library, we can avoid the crowd and head towards the police station!"

Brian Brackbrick and George Bum ran towards the crowd and ducked into an alleyway just before the first people reached it.

"But we still have the medals, Brian!" George pointed out. "Won't they all just follow us?"

"Precisely, George! To the police station!"

CHAPTER 2:

THE MEDALS

Brian Brackbrick and George Bum arrived at the police station and ran straight inside. There was no-one at the counter or in the small waiting area – Sergeant Shelley Shiplap was, of course, among the hypnotised crowd outside, slowly shuffling their way towards them.

It was quiet in the police station, but voices could be heard from down the corridor that led to the cells. It sounded like people arguing.

"What are we doing here, Brian?" George asked. "We need to get rid of these medals!"

"Yes, indeed, George, and there is the perfect place!" Brian replied, pointing down the corridor.

"But the cells are down there!" said a worried George. "That's where Carl Scorpion is – and Raymond Rings – and Harry Hatman!"

"Do not forget Morris Hawkwind! I believe we can rescue him, get rid of these medals, and teach those villains a lesson!"

"Are you sure, Brian?"

"Quite sure, yes," Brian said he reached behind the counter and took something. "I am the one-hundred-and-thirty-eighth cleverest person in the world, after all. Let us go."

Brian and George walked along the dimly-lit corridor towards the cells, knowing that they did not have much time until the shuffling crowd reached the police station.

The sounds of arguing became louder as Brian and George approached the cells, and they heard some familiar voices.

There were three cells along the corridor.

Sitting on their bunks in the first cell were Harry Hatman and Carl Scorpion. Harry Hatman's enormous cowboy hat had been confiscated, revealing a huge bald patch on the back of his head.

In the next cell was Morris Hawkwind, who was arguing with the occupant of the last cell, Raymond Rings. Brian and George were relieved to see that Morris Hawkwind seemed to be okay.

"I thought you were my friend, man!" Morris Hawkwind shouted at Raymond Rings. "You weren't interested in the music, man, you just wanted to ruin Hawkwind Radio and set me up!"

"Oh calm down, yes, calm down," said Raymond Rings, who seemed to be thoroughly bored by the argument. "It's a shame you couldn't work with us, yes, with us."

"I'm not working for that Sparker dude, man!" said Morris Hawkwind.

"Sparker? Sparker? I'll give you Sparker, you bedraggled waste of space!" shouted Carl Scorpion, who seemed to be scowling harder than ever. "Just you wait until Mr. Sparker turns up to let us out! Well, well, look who it is!"

The four people in the cells all turned to look at Brian Brackbrick and George Bum.

"Brian! George!" called Morris Hawkwind, who was very pleased to see them. "Are you guys okay? You know all that stuff with Hawkwind Radio wasn't me, right? It was him, man!"

Morris Hawkwind pointed at Raymond Rings, who rolled his eyes.

"We know, Mr. Hawkwind – I mean, Morris," said George Bum. "We're here to let you out."

"Let him out? Let him out? Just how do you plan to do that, brats?" growled Carl Scorpion.

"With these, Mr. Scorpion," Brian replied as he held up the set of keys he had taken from behind the counter.

Carl Scorpion, Harry Hatman and Raymond Rings all looked shocked as Brian Brackbrick unlocked Morris Hawkwind's cell and let him out into the corridor.

"Oy, brats!" shouted Carl Scorpion. "You can't do that! Where are you going?"

"Do not worry, Mr. Scorpion, you will have company soon enough!" said Brian, taking the medal from around his neck.

"We don't have much time!" George pointed out as he also removed his medal.

Suddenly there was a great deal of noise coming from the entrance to the police station – the crowd of people had arrived, and were slowly shuffling in!

"What's going on, man?" asked a confused Morris Hawkwind.

"We will explain on the way, Mr. Hawkwind," replied Brian. "Now, George!"

Just as the first people in the crowd had almost reached them, Brian Brackbrick shoved his medal through the bars of Raymond Rings' cell, and it clattered to the floor. George Bum did the same with his medal, which clanged on to the floor of Harry Hatman and Carl Scorpion's cell.

"Let us go!" shouted Brian, and they ran to the far end of the corridor, unlocked the side door using the keys from the counter, and ran out into the street.

As they left, they heard the shouts and cries of Harry Hatman, Raymond Rings, and Carl Scorpion, as all the hypnotised people of the town filled up the corridor and the inside of the police station...

CHAPTER 3:

A SCORPION

IN A LUNCHBOX

Brian Brackbrick, George Bum and Morris Hawkwind ran out of the police station, down the main street, and did not stop until they had reached the music shop.

While they got their breath back, all three looked back up the street to see if anyone was following them.

"Phew, no-one is following us," said George Bum.

"Indeed not," replied Brian. "Hopefully they will be kept busy at the police station."

"What's happened to this town, man?" asked Morris Hawkwind. "Everyone's gone crazy!"

Brian and George quickly explained to a shocked Morris Hawkwind all that had happened since his arrest.

"I can't believe all this, man!" said Morris Hawkwind.

"It's true, Mr. Hawkwind – I mean, Morris," insisted George.

"George and I must go, Mr. Hawkwind," said Brian. "We have some things we need to pick up."

"Will you be okay, dudes?"

"We'll be fine," said George. "We have a plan."

"You must do something here in the music shop, Mr. Hawkwind," added Brian. "We will come back for you later."

"For sure, man, if you're sure," said Morris Hawkwind. "What is it you want me to do?"

"Mr. Sparker is controlling everyone using the control rings, and Raymond Rings' jewellery," Brian explained. "I do not think that the jewellery is powerful enough on its own –

HAWKWIND RADIO

I suspect **RADIO** has been switched back on. If it has, you must switch it off again."

"Oh, man! Not that again!" said Morris Hawkwind. "I knew we should have taken all those speakers down!"

"Nonsense," Brian insisted. "The speakers are not the problem, it is the people misusing them."

"I suppose, man," said Morris Hawkwind. "But how will I get in? Sergeant Shiplap told me it was all locked up."

"Someone has been in the music shop in a hurry," explained Brian. "I think you will find that the door is not locked."

Morris Hawkwind tried the music shop door, and it opened. "Later, dudes! Be careful!"

Brian and George ran off to the end of the street, around the corner and through the front door of Brian's house.

"What do we need to pick up?" asked George.

"There are a number of things that may be useful tonight. One is in the music shop; three are in the library; and three of them are right here!"

Brian Brackbrick grabbed his backpack and ran upstairs, with George Bum following close behind.

"The first thing we need is our little friend, Simon the scorpion!" Brian said as he carefully placed Simon in the travel case they had made for him – an old lunchbox, with air-holes in the lid, and small twigs and leaves inside.

"What else do we need?"

"We need the fruit of the Eastern Mini Squirt-Ball Orange Fruit Plant," answered Brian, pointing to the small pot plant with tiny orange-coloured fruit sitting on the windowsill.

"The fruit we've been using to train Simon?" George asked as he plucked a few of the orange-coloured fruit from the plant and placed them in a smaller plastic container.

"Yes, indeed." Brian placed Simon's travel case and the plastic container in his backpack. "Simon has been well trained, but other scorpions will not be able to resist these little fruit."

As they were about to leave, Brian Brackbrick reached to the back of a shelf and retrieved the third item they needed – the woolly hat from Harry Hatman's shop. "This may also come in handy. Let us go, George! Next stop, the library!"

CHAPTER 4:

OLD FRIENDS IN

THE LIBRARY

Brian Brackbrick and George Bum walked along the main street towards the library, where Spencer Sparker had so dramatically revealed himself. There was no sign of him now, and the area around the library was quiet and deserted. It was now getting dark, and this, combined with the unusual silence, made their journey seem rather spooky.

Something must have happened in the police station, as a few of the hypnotised people of the town were now shuffling out of the entrance and back onto the street. Now they had got rid of the medals, Brian and George only had to make sure that they were not seen or heard, so they moved quickly and quietly from doorway to doorway until they had reached the library.

Just outside the library, Brian stopped – there was their friend Fancy Nancy Sprinkle from the cake shop, shuffling across the road. Brian waited until Nancy turned and saw them and started slowly walking over towards them.

Once they were certain that Nancy would follow them inside, Brian and George walked through the door of the library.

"You must distract Nancy when she comes in," Brian whispered to George.

"Okay, Brian, if you're sure."

"Quite sure, yes, do not worry. Here she comes!" said Brian as he moved away from the door.

Fancy Nancy stumbled in through the door with her arms outstretched and a blank look on her face. Like all the other hypnotised people, Nancy was wearing Raymond Rings' matching jewellery – earrings, necklace and bracelets.

"Over here, Nancy! Yoo-hoo! Over here!" waved George Bum, who really really hoped that Brian knew what he was doing and would be able to help Nancy.

As Nancy slowly moved towards the waving George, Brian sneaked up behind her and carefully placed something on her neck.

Nancy kept on going, getting closer to George…

"Yoo-hoo, Nancy!" George called out. "Brian, it's not working!"

"Just a moment, George," Brian reassured him.

Nancy got closer and closer to George Bum, until her outstretched hands could almost grab him… and then she stopped. "Ow," Nancy said, and she slowly fell to the floor.

"That was close, Brian," said a relieved George as he found a cushion and placed it under Nancy's head. "Will she be okay?"

"Yes, George," said Brian as he lowered his hand for Simon the scorpion to climb onto. "Simon is still a baby Very Rare Purple Spotted Scorpion, so Nancy will only sleep for an hour."

"So should we take the jewellery off while she's sleeping?"

"Precisely!" said Brian, as he gave Simon the scorpion a tiny orange-coloured fruit as a reward.

"Wait a moment – did you hear that?"

George Bum listened, and heard a voice, like someone muttering to themselves somewhere in the library. "Someone else is in here, Brian!"

Being very careful not to make any noise, Brian and George followed the sound of the voice to see…the librarian, Dr. Harley Letters!

Dr. Letters was hypnotised, just like Nancy, but he was standing in front of a shelf marked *Jewellery and Rings of the World*, saying to himself, over and over again, "Ring…find the ring…get the ring…the ring…"

"Is he okay, Brian?"

"Yes, I believe so," said Brian, who smiled as he carefully placed Simon the scorpion on Dr. Harley Letters' neck. "Mr. Sparker told all the hypnotised people to 'get the ring'. I believe that our friend Dr. Letters is fighting Mr. Sparker's control in his own way."

"Ring…find the ring…get the ring…the – ow!" said Dr. Letters, and he slowly fell to the floor.

"What should we do now, Brian?"

"Well, we should make Dr. Letters comfortable. After that, we should carefully remove his watch and all of Nancy's jewellery. I am sure they will both be fine when they wake up."

"What should we do while we wait?" George Bum asked as he picked up Simon the scorpion.

"We must search the library, for three books that we will need," said Brian Brackbrick.

"To the bookshelves!"

CHAPTER 5:

RAYMOND RINGS AND THE WOOLLY HAT

An hour later, both Fancy Nancy and Dr. Harley Letters woke up and slowly got to their feet.

"Where am I? What's happened?" asked a confused Nancy.

"Goodness me, what a lovely refreshing nap," said Dr. Letters as he stretched. "Hello, you two!"

"We're glad you're both okay, Dr. Letters," said a relieved George Bum.

"What am I doing in the library? Where's all my jewellery?" asked Nancy.

Brian Brackbrick and George Bum quickly explained everything to Dr. Letters and Nancy, telling them all that had happened.

"Well, I say!" said a shocked Dr. Letters. "Raymond Rings has been working for Mr. Sparker all along! Terrible business."

"Yes, indeed, Dr. Letters," agreed Brian.

"Mr. Sparker has used the whole town, like every one of us is just a toy for him to play with," said Nancy seriously. "I hope you two are going to stop him."

"Of course, Nancy," said Brian. "I have a plan."

"Brian is the one-hundred and thirty-eighth cleverest person in the world, after all," added George.

"What can we do to help?" asked Dr. Letters.

Brian handed him three books. "Take these books, go to the cake shop, and prepare the Super Giant Mega Cake Mixer. Be careful that you are not seen or followed."

"The Super Giant Mega Cake Mixer!" said a shocked Nancy. "Are you sure, Brian? I haven't used that since – "

"Quite sure, yes," said Brian. "We will meet you there."

They all left the library, with Dr. Letters and Nancy setting out for the cake shop, and the two boys heading back to the music shop to meet Morris Hawkwind.

Inside the music shop, Morris Hawkwind was panicking.

"Dudes! I can't switch it off! I can't stop it!" shouted Morris Hawkwind.

"What's happened, Mr. Hawkwind – I mean, Morris?" asked George Bum.

"You were right, the transmitter for **HAWKWIND RADIO** has been switched on, but I can't make it stop! Look!" Morris Hawkwind took Brian and George through to the back room, and pointed at the transmitter in the corner. All the lights on the transmitter box were blinking, and it was making a humming sound.

"Have you tried unplugging it, Mr. Hawkwind?" Brian asked.

"For sure, man!" said Morris Hawkwind. "I've switched it off, unplugged it, kicked it, shouted rude words at it, nothing works!"

"It is a signal!" said Brian, who was reminded of a similar-looking box in Raymond Rings' secret workshop... "There is another transmitter beaming a signal to this one."

George Bum's eyes lit up with understanding. "In the jewellery shop, Brian! When we were trapped in the secret workshop!"

"That is correct! It seems that Raymond Rings has been very busy indeed."

"What do you mean, dudes?" asked a puzzled Morris Hawkwind.

"George and I must go next door to the jewellery shop," explained Brian. "Wait here until the signal stops, then switch everything off and meet us in the cake shop. You must take the Giant Alpine Horn with you."

"The Giant Alpine Horn? Are you sure, man? That's, like, really heavy."

"Quite sure, yes," said Brian Brackbrick. "Do not forget it! Let us go, George!"

Brian and George ran to the jewellery shop next door, opened the giant metal door of the secret workshop using the control ring, and went inside. There in the corner was a black box with flashing lights on the front, exactly like a bigger version of Morris Hawkwind's transmitter.

"There it is, Brian! Let's switch it off!"

The lights on the transmitter, however, kept on flashing, even after it had been unplugged.

"What a surprise, yes, surprise," said a voice from the doorway, as Raymond Rings stepped into the workshop. "I really must stop leaving this door open, yes, open."

"How did you escape from the police station, Mr. Rings?" asked George.

"Oh, your nasty little trick backfired, yes, backfired. The police station can't hold all those people. They broke the doors down to get to those medals, yes, medals."

"You must switch this transmitter off, Mr. Rings!" insisted Brian.

"Oh, it can't be switched off now, it's too late, yes, too late!" said Raymond Rings. "The signal will go on broadcasting forever, keeping the whole town under Mr. Sparker's control, yes, control!"

"If we cannot switch it off, we must block the signal another way!" Brian took out the woolly hat from his backpack – the special woolly hat from Harry Hatman's shop, full of wires and twiddly bits – the woolly hat that Brian had fixed to block out all sound! Could it also block this signal? Brian quickly placed the hat over the transmitter, stretching it to cover the whole box.

"No! Yes, no!" shouted Raymond Rings in distress as he ran over to the transmitter.

Brian and George seized their chance and ran out of the secret workshop, closing the door and locking it with the control ring.

"No! Let me out, yes, out!" shouted Raymond Rings through the metal door. "The door won't open, yes, open! Mr. Sparker needs me, yes, needs me!"

"I am afraid Mr. Sparker will have to do without you, Mr. Rings," Brian called out as they left the jewellery shop. "Goodbye, yes, goodbye!"

As they stepped out onto the pavement, George Bum looked down the street and saw a figure wearing an enormous cowboy hat, a hat that was so big it looked ridiculous…

"Look, Brian! It's Harry Hatman!"

The figure wearing the enormous hat walked into Old Mr. Hatston's hat shop.

"Yes, indeed, George. Let us see what Mr. Hatman has to say about all this…"

CHAPTER 6:

HARRY HATMAN DOES NOT KNOW WHEN TO SHUT UP

Brian Brackbrick and George Bum followed Harry Hatman into the hat shop. Inside, a large space had been cleared in the middle of the shop floor for piles of boxes, which Harry Hatman was bringing through from the back room.

"Heyyyyyyyyyy!" said Harry Hatman in a surprisingly cheery voice, as he set down another box. "What are you guys doing here?"

"We're here to stop you, Mr. Hatman!" said George Bum.

"Ha! Great sense of humour you got there," laughed Harry Hatman, his gigantic hat wobbling on his head. "No-one can stop Mr. Sparker now!"

"Perhaps you are right, Mr. Hatman," said Brian thoughtfully.

"There you go, that's the spirit!" said Harry Hatman. "Why spend all your energy fighting us? It won't be so bad after Mr. Sparker has – whoops, better not say too much, ha ha!"

"Mr. Sparker must be very clever indeed, to plan all of this," said Brian.

"Clever?" said Harry Hatman. "Oh man, that guy knows everything!"

"But Mr. Sparker couldn't have done all of this without you, Mr. Hatman," added George. "You must be very important to him."

"Well, yes, sure," said Harry Hatman proudly. "We all are. What a team! Me, with all the mind-controlling hats; the jewellery guy, with all the hypnotic jewellery, and the rings, and the radio stuff he took from the music guy…"

"Do not forget Mr. Scorpion," said Brian.

"Oh yeah, the scorpion guy!" said Harry Hatman. "Between you and me, he's kind of mean, but he knows his stuff! He's got all those scorpions boxed up and ready to be shipped out!"

"What are these boxes for, Mr. Hatman?" asked George Bum.

"These are my special hats, of course! All different styles and colours, for everyone to wear, all over the world!"

"All over the world, Mr. Hatman?" Brian asked, trying to keep him talking.

"Oh, sure! Mr. Sparker's only using this town as a test, like a trial run! Now we know all the stuff works, all the hats, jewellery, scorpions and speakers can be sent out all over the world! I'll be delivering the first lot of hats tonight!"

"This is all very interesting, Mr. Hatman," said Brian.

"See, I knew you guys were okay!" said Harry Hatman. "Why don't you work with us, instead of against us?"

"Maybe we could help you carry the boxes out from the back room?" George suggested.

"That's a great idea! Let's go!" said Harry Hatman, and he led Brian and George into the back room.

The back room of the hat shop was still packed full of boxes, both Old Mr. Hatston's dusty and faded boxes, and Harry Hatman's brand new boxes filled with mind-controlling hats. Some of the piles of boxes went all the way up to the ceiling, and looked very precarious, like they could easily fall...

Harry Hatman walked in between these teetering piles of boxes and bent down to pick up a box.

"Now, George!" Brian Brackbrick shouted, and they both reached up, grabbed the edge of Harry Hatman's enormous hat, and pulled down as hard as they could.

The hat became wedged over Harry Hatman's face, and stuck fast.

"Mmmm mmmm mmmm!" shouted Harry Hatman, his voice muffled by the hat.

Brian and George each pushed over as many piles of boxes as they could, and everything fell down and piled up on top of Harry Hatman.

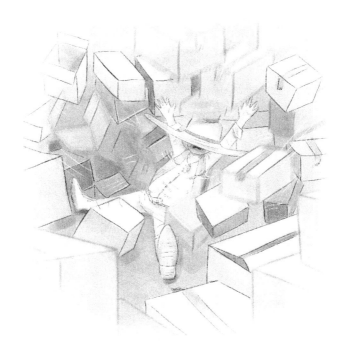

"You will not be delivering any hats tonight, Mr. Hatman!" Brian called over his shoulder as the two boys ran out of the shop.

"Should we meet everyone at the cake shop now, Brian?"

"Not yet! Mr. Hatman was kind enough to tell us Mr. Sparker's plan. We have already stopped Raymond Rings by trapping him in his secret workshop, and Mr. Hatman is stuck under all those boxes, but there is still one other person."

"Do you mean – " said a worried George Bum.

"Yes, George… Mr. Carl Scorpion!"

CHAPTER 7:
CARL SCORPION
GETS A TASTE OF
HIS OWN MEDICINE

Brian Brackbrick and George Bum ran across the road to the pet shop, briefly stopping outside to remove Simon the scorpion's travel case from the backpack.

As Brian carefully held Simon the scorpion in his hand so that he could not be seen, the sounds of an argument came from inside the pet shop.

"What are you doing with all these boxes? Ooh, I don't want any more of these things in here!"

It was Frankie Featherface! It seemed that the hypnotic signal had indeed been switched off, as Frankie Featherface was back to normal – but who was he talking to?

"Things? Things? I'll give you things, Featherface!" shouted Carl Scorpion.

Brian and George stepped into the pet shop, much to the relief of Frankie Featherface. "Ooh, thank goodness you're here!"

"We are pleased to see you are not hypnotised any longer, Mr. Featherface," said Brian.

"Hypnotised? What do you mean?" asked Frankie Featherface. "Ooh, I think I must have been daydreaming. Suddenly it was dark and I was outside the shop – and he was in here!"

"I don't know how you've turned that signal off, brats," said Carl Scorpion menacingly, "but you've interfered for the last time."

"What are you doing with all these boxes, Mr. Scorpion?" asked George.

"Never you mind, brat! That's Mr. Sparker's business!" said Carl Scorpion.

In the middle of the shop floor were piles of boxes and crates, each one labelled:

VERY RARE PURPLE
SPOTTED SCORPIONS

The plastic crates were see-through, and the yellow-green and purple-spotted scorpions inside were rather large, and fully grown.

"Mr. Sparker's plan has failed, Mr. Scorpion!" Brian responded. "Oh, I say, I suddenly need to tie my shoelace."

Brian pretended to tie his shoelace – he was actually wearing sandals, but no-one noticed! Unseen by everyone, Brian released Simon the scorpion onto the floor.

"Plan? Plan? I'll give you plan, brats! What do you know about Mr. Sparker's plan, eh?"

"We know that Raymond Rings is trapped in his workshop, and won't be delivering any special jewellery tonight," said George Bum. Carl Scorpion scowled.

"We also know that Harry Hatman is now trapped under a pile of boxes in the back room of the hat shop," added Brian.

Carl Scorpion scowled so hard it looked like his face might crack; he did not notice that Simon the scorpion had scuttled across the floor, climbed onto his shoe, and was now climbing up the outside of his trousers...

"Brats!" he shouted. "You've ruined everything! I was going to leave you for Mr. Sparker, but now I'll deal with you myself!"

Carl Scorpion bent down and removed the lids from all the plastic crates, laughing as a swarm of fully-grown Very Rare Purple Spotted Scorpions climbed out of the crates and made their way down the piles of boxes.

"Oh no, scorpions!" shouted a panicking Frankie Featherface.

"Do not move, Mr. Featherface!" Brian called out.

The scorpions made their way across the shop floor towards them, like a yellow-green and purple wave of legs and claws and stingers.

"Ooh, they're getting closer!" cried Frankie Featherface.

Carl Scorpion felt something crawling on his neck, and stopped laughing.

The scorpions got closer.

Carl Scorpion reached up to his neck and felt something sticky that smelt like oranges.

Just as the first scorpion reached Brian Brackbrick's shoe, all the scorpions suddenly stopped. Then, as one, they all turned and rushed back towards Carl Scorpion!

"No! What have you done? Noooo!" shouted Carl Scorpion, as all the adult Very Rare Purple Spotted Scorpions climbed up his legs, inside his shirt, all over his arms, his neck, and his face. Very soon he was completely covered in the scorpions, which became annoyed and started to sting, over and over again.

Carl Scorpion **fell** to the floor.

Frankie Featherface, who had been hiding his face behind his hands, now peeked through his fingers. "Ooh, is he okay?"

"Yes, but he will sleep for a very long time," Brian answered with a grin.

"I don't understand," said Frankie Featherface. "What happened to all the scorpions?"

"This!" said Brian, holding up one of the tiny fruit of the Eastern Mini Squirt-Ball Orange Fruit Plant. "Scorpions cannot resist it, unless they are well-trained and very clever indeed."

Brian bent down to pick up Simon the scorpion, who had made his way back across the shop floor, and gave him the fruit as a reward.

"Once our little friend had squeezed the fruit onto Carl Scorpion, all the other scorpions just could not help themselves," he explained.

"We have to go now, Mr. Featherface," said George Bum. "Can you stay here and make sure all the scorpions stay here where it's safe?"

"Me? Stay here? On my own?" said a terrified Frankie Featherface.

"You will be fine, Mr. Featherface," Brian reassured him. "As long as you do not move too quickly. Let us go, George! We must deal with Mr. Sparker, once and for all!"

CHAPTER 8:

NANCY'S SPECIAL MIX

Brian Brackbrick and George Bum made their way across the street and into the cake shop, where they were pleased to see Fancy Nancy, Dr. Letters and Morris Hawkwind waiting for them.

"I do hope you know what you're doing, Brian!" shouted Nancy above the noise of the Super Giant Mega Cake Mixer. The huge mixer on the floor was the size of a washing machine, and it was churning, clanging and bouncing from side to side. It was a very old machine, and was battered and dented, and smudged with mysterious stains and marks and scratches.

"Of course, Nancy, do not worry."

Morris Hawkwind and Dr. Letters had moved the Giant Alpine Horn into position, so that the mouthpiece of the instrument connected to the Mixer. The rest of the Giant Alpine Horn curved down to the floor and then back up, pointing out into the middle of the shop.

"Are you sure about this, man?" asked Morris Hawkwind.

"Quite sure, yes," said Brian.

Nancy was not sure at all, but she kept quiet while she continued to stack up huge piles of her pink t-shirts on the floor next to the counter.

Brian and George sat down on the marshmallow cushions next to the table that was shaped like a giant cake with white and green icing. It had been a long night, and both had to struggle not to fall asleep.

"Well, we have followed your instructions, chaps," said Dr. Letters, holding up three books. "These books have certainly proved to be useful."

The three books from the library were:

- an instruction book (called *Quick-Setting Cement for Emergency Repairs*);
- a cookery book (called *Cupcake Mixing Made Easy*);
- and a comic book called *Captain Awesome versus the Glue-Man*).

"Sure, if it all works, man!" said a worried Morris Hawkwind.

"It will work, do not worry," said Brian.

"Thank you for all your help," added George.

"Anytime, dudes," said Morris Hawkwind.

"Happy to help," said Dr. Letters.

"I really don't know about this, boys," said Nancy, shaking her head. "The last time I used the Super Giant Mega Cake Mixer…I caused the Yoghurt Inferno! Such a terrible mess. What if that happens again?"

"I am counting on it, Nancy," said Brian Brackbrick. "In a few moments, Mr. Sparker will burst through that door, and we will need something to stop him with."

"How on earth can you be so sure of that, Brian?" asked Dr. Letters.

"Because of **this!**" said Brian, holding up the

gold ring.

"Is that the ring that Mr. Sparker wanted?" asked Nancy.

"Yes, Nancy," said George Bum. "It's the last control ring that Mr. Sparker needs."

"Oh, I say, well played, chaps," said Dr. Letters.

"By now, Mr. Sparker will have realised that we have switched off the radio signal and stopped Raymond Rings, Harry Hatman and Carl Scorpion," explained Brian. "He will be more desperate than ever to reclaim this ring. It is his last chance to succeed."

Brian Brackbrick felt the ring start to hum, so he slipped it onto his finger and closed his hand tightly around it so that it would not fall off.

Just then, the door to the cake shop flew open, and a loud, booming voice echoed around the shop.

"BRACKBRICK!!!" shouted an enraged Spencer Sparker...

CHAPTER 9:

A CUPCAKE INFERNO

Mr. Spencer Sparker stepped into the cake shop, looking rather scruffy and dishevelled. His smart Mayor's robe was now dirty and torn, and his face was red and blotchy from where he had torn off the fake beard disguise. The special Mayor's hat with flashing lights did not look so impressive now, with some of the lights broken and a big tear along the side.

Above all else, though, Mr. Sparker looked very, very cross indeed.

"You have been very busy boys, it seems," said Mr. Sparker. "Raymond Rings is **trapped,** Carl Scorpion is asleep, and I can't find Hatman anywhere!"

Dr. Letters, Nancy and Morris Hawkwind stood motionless, afraid to move.

"To make matters worse," continued Mr. Sparker, "all those pathetic people outside are no longer under my control! Some of them even attacked me! How dare they!"

"We're not frightened of you!" shouted Nancy, who was very frightened indeed. "You can't treat the good people of this town like that, we won't let you!"

"You people are insects under my feet," said Mr. Sparker menacingly, "and this town belongs to me now. Once I have that ring, I will not be stopped!"

"I'll **never** let you have this ring!" said George, holding his hands behind his back.

"You are brave, George Bum, but you cannot **fool** me so easily," said Mr. Sparker. "You do not have the ring. **He does.**"

Mr. Sparker raised his hands towards Brian Brackbrick. The rings on each of Mr. Sparker's fingers – except one – began to **hum** loudly.

Brian felt his own hand **stretch** out in front of him, and he felt an enormous **pull** towards Mr. Sparker, as if an invisible rope was **tugging** him closer and closer.

Brian tried to pull against it, but it was no good; the ring began to **slip** from his finger…

"GIVE IT TO ME!" shouted Mr. Sparker.

The ring flew from Brian's finger, shot through the air and landed on Mr. Sparker's one empty finger. All the lights on the special Mayor's hat that still worked seemed to glow brighter and crackle with energy.

"NOW, NANCY!" shouted Brian.

Things happened very quickly after this.

Nancy reached down and pulled the lever on the front of the Super Giant Mega Cake Mixer. The noisy machine stopped bouncing from side to side and made a whooshing sound instead.

Mr. Sparker laughed loudly.

Nancy, Dr. Letters and Morris Hawkwind dived for cover behind the piles of pink t-shirts on the floor.

Mr. Sparker carried on laughing loudly, and raised his hands up, the control rings glowing with energy.

Nancy's special mix – made to Brian Brackbrick's instructions – came flooding out of the Super Giant Mega Cake Mixer and into the mouthpiece of the Giant Alpine Horn. The giant instrument trembled and shook as the special mix made its way to the other end of the horn, pointing out into the middle of the shop.

Realising something was wrong, Mr. Sparker stopped laughing.

Brian Brackbrick and George Bum jumped onto the table that was shaped like a giant cake with white and green icing. Luckily, the table shaped like a giant cake was, in fact, actually a giant cake, and they fell through layers of green and white icing, yellow sponge, thick cream and bright red strawberry jam.

Mr. Sparker turned to look at the end of the Giant Alpine Horn, just as the special mix roared out of

it and splattered all over him, completely
covering him.

Brian and George clambered out from the remains of the cake and fled through the door of the cake shop into the street. Mr. Sparker, covered in the special mix which was already beginning to set, stomped after them.

The people in the town turned to watch in amazement as Brian and George, covered in icing, sponge, cream and jam, ran up the street towards the library, knocking over a surprised Charlie Chipchase on their way.

Mr. Sparker followed, getting slower and slower as the special mix covering him hardened, looking like a shambling cupcake monster.

Brian and George reached the doors of the library, and turned to watch as Mr. Sparker clomped and squelched towards them.

As Mr. Sparker got close, he reached out a squidgy hand towards Brian Brackbrick, and the special mix finally set, as hard as concrete, freezing him in place.

Brian Brackbrick and George Bum breathed a sigh of relief, and started to wipe off the icing, sponge, cream and jam.

"Evening all!" came a voice from beside the frozen form of Spencer Sparker. "You're under arrest, Lord Mayor Spencer, Mr. Sparker, or whatever your name is at the moment!" said Sergeant Shelley Shiplap. "Let's be having you! Come along with me at once!"

"I do not think that will be necessary, Sergeant Shiplap," said Brian. "Mr. Sparker will not be going anywhere, and he will not trouble the town again."

"Goodness me," said Dr. Harley Letters, who had now caught up and was looking in amazement at the frozen form of Mr. Sparker. "I've always said the library needed a statue, but this is not quite what I meant!"

CHAPTER 10:

BRIAN BRACKBRICK AND GEORGE BUM DO <u>NOT</u> RECEIVE A MEDAL

The next day, after everyone had had a good sleep, all the people of the town gathered in front of the library, where the statue of Mr. Sparker stood.

It had been decided to leave the statue where it was, as a reminder of everything that had happened. A few pigeons had already left their own mark on Mr. Sparker's head.

Dr. Harley Letters stepped out in front of the crowd, with Brian Brackbrick and George Bum following behind him.

"Welcome, everyone," said Dr. Letters. "I think you will all agree, we owe a huge debt of gratitude to young Brian Brackbrick and young George Bum. Well done, chaps."

Dr. Letters shook their hands while everyone cheered and clapped. Mr. and Mrs. Brackbrick and Mr. and Mrs. Bum looked on proudly.

"I hope you don't mind, chaps," continued Dr. Letters, "but after recent events, I will certainly not be giving you medals!" Everyone in the crowd laughed.

"There is, of course, still a great deal of cleaning up and sorting out to do," Dr. Letters reminded everyone. "Harry Hatman, Carl Scorpion and Raymond Rings must be taken to a proper prison as soon as possible."

"Evening all!" called out Sergeant Shiplap from the crowd. "I'll sort that out straight away!"

"Also, Nancy's cake shop is a terrible mess," said Dr. Letters.

"That's no problem!" called out Nancy. "I cleaned up after the Yoghurt Inferno, I can clean up after this too!"

"We'll help you, Nancy," said George Bum.

"My heroes!" said Nancy, which made George blush just a little.

"There are boxes and crates of dangerous scorpions to deal with," said Dr. Letters. "Perhaps we can find a ZOO that can look after them."

"Ooh, I'm not going near those things again!" called out Frankie Featherface.

"They are only dangerous if you do not look after them properly, Mr. Featherface," Brian explained. "We will help you with that, too."

"So, there is lots to do," said Dr. Letters, "but I think we should take a moment to thank these two young fellows for all their hard work."

Everyone cheered again, and Brian Brackbrick and George Bum spent a long time shaking everyone's hands and being thanked for all their efforts. Their town was safe, Mr. Sparker had been stopped for good, and all was well with the world.

EPILOGUE

A few weeks later…

Brian Brackbrick arrived home from school to find that a letter had been delivered for him.

"There's a letter for you on the table, Brian!" called out Mr. Brackbrick. "It looks important!"

The envelope was addressed:

To: **Brian Brackbrick**
(No. 138)

Realising what it must be, Brian excitedly opened the envelope. Inside was a letter, and an invitation card.

The invitation card read:

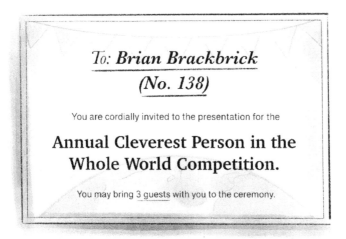

To: **Brian Brackbrick**
(No. 138)

You are cordially invited to the presentation for the

Annual Cleverest Person in the Whole World Competition.

You may bring 3 guests with you to the ceremony.

The date on the invitation was the following week – just before his eleventh birthday!

This was terribly exciting. Brian Brackbrick had been taking part in the competition for several years, even though he was only ten years old, gradually getting higher and higher on the list. Only the top two-hundred and fifty were invited to attend the ceremony.

Brian eagerly read the letter to find out his new place on the list of cleverest people in the whole world.

The letter read:

```
Dear Brian Brackbrick,

It is with great pleasure that we write
to inform you of your new position in
the list of Cleverest People in the
Whole World.

Your position this year is: 105

This means that you are the one-hundred
and fifth cleverest person in the whole
world. Congratulations!
```

Brian Brackbrick was very happy indeed. The one-hundred and fifth cleverest person in the whole world – this was incredible!

After a moment, however, Brian carried on reading.

The rest of the letter read:

Many congratulations to the new number one on the list –

The CLEVEREST PERSON IN THE WHOLE WORLD is:

SIDNEY SIDESTRAND

Brian was surprised.

Usually, the list was made up of names that he recognised from past ceremonies, and the number one on the list was always a familiar name.

Not this time, though.

Brian Brackbrick said quietly, mostly to himself:

"Who is Sidney Sidestrand...?"

A WORD FROM
BRIAN BRACKBRICK

Hello readers!

I am very pleased indeed that you have carried on reading about my adventures, and you have been with me and George all the way!

We have stopped Mr. Sparker and his villainous friends, and everything will go back to normal now. Or will it...?

A WORD FROM
BRIAN BRACKBRICK

I wonder if George and I should investigate who this 'Sidney Sidestrand' fellow is?

Perhaps we will, and I hope you will join us again — look out for our next adventures!

A WORD FROM
BRIAN BRACKBRICK

If you would like to send me a message, please do!

You can email me –

brianbrackbrick@gmail.com

– or message me on social media:

@BrianBrackbrick

(Twitter/Instagram)

Keep reading!

Brian Brackbrick

ABOUT THE AUTHOR

GR Dix is a scientist in his day job, and a writer of children's books at all other times! He is a late starter as an author, but has been a fan of books, comics and reading his whole life.

The major influences on his writing are (in no particular order) Roald Dahl, Simon Furman, Stephen King and Terry Pratchett.

An active member of the Society of Children's Book Writers and Illustrators (SCBWI), he attends events, conferences and critique meetings as much as possible.

GR Dix lives in the UK, and credits his success to the unfailing support of his wife, family and network of close friends.

You can contact GR Dix through his Facebook page (GR Dix Author), or on Twitter (@GRDixAuthor), where you can find the latest news and updates.